TROLL AT THE TRAIN STATION

Gilbert,

Much love from

Grandma!

♡ Bridget Snorte

ALSO FORTHCOMING BY **BRIDGET SPROULS**

Gnome at the Laundromat

TROLL AT THE TRAIN STATION

Written and Illustrated by
Bridget Sprouls

First Published 2017 by Bridget Sprouls
Ship Bottom, NJ 08008
BridgetSprouls@gmail.com

ISBN-13: 978-1979176330
ISBN-10: 1979176337

For Onalee

You can learn a lot about trolls
by watching one at the train station.

Trolls don't like having to wait,
so they often try changing the departure times
on the big timetable.

Trolls love giving an activity their full attention and aren't easily distracted.

As forest creatures, trolls are very good
at blending in to the scenery.

Think twice before asking a troll for directions.
In troll culture, shouting is thought to be polite....

...So is cutting in line.

Troll eyes glow in the dark like lamps.

Once on the train, trolls are too large to fit in one seat. But they can manage with three.

To make the most of a short train ride,
a troll may trim his enormous toenails
(and hopefully pass one off as a ticket).

In the old days, trolls lived slow, peaceful lives.
They miss those days.

Finally, trolls are heavy sleepers.
Unless they stay awake, they may wind up
right back where they started.

Made in the USA
Columbia, SC
02 May 2018